The DONKEY'S DREAM

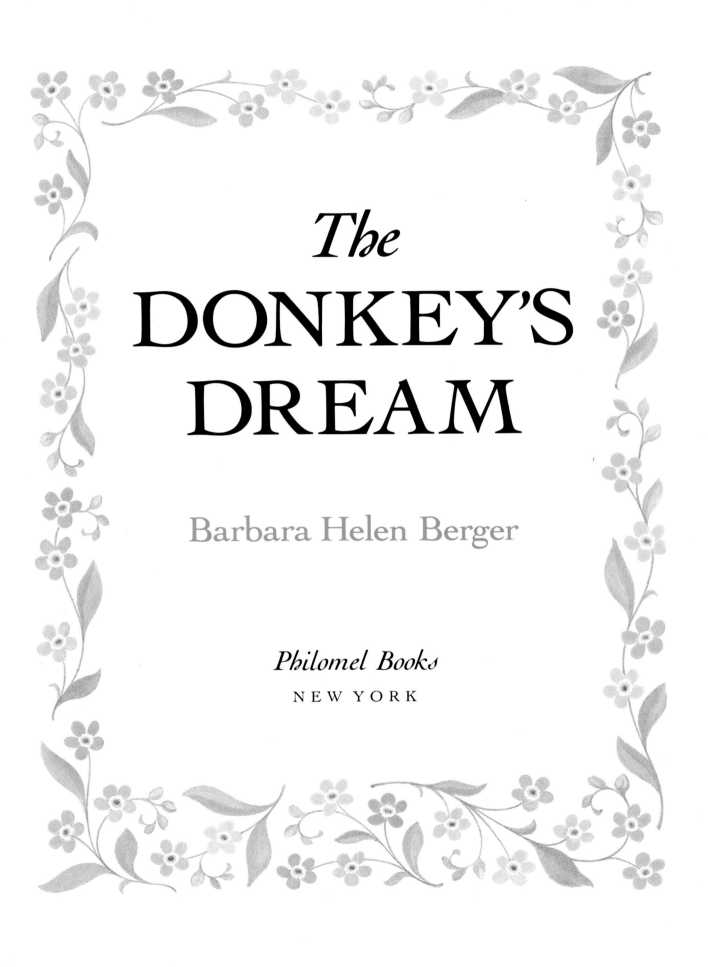

The DONKEY'S DREAM

Barbara Helen Berger

Philomel Books

NEW YORK

Published in 1985 by Philomel Books,
a division of The Putnam & Grosset Group,
200 Madison Avenue, New York, NY 10016.
Published simultaneously in Canada.
Sandcastle Books and the Sandcastle logo are trademarks
belonging to The Putnam & Grosset Group. Printed in Hong Kong by
South China Printing Co. (1988) Ltd.

Library of Congress Cataloging-in-Publication Data
Berger, Barbara.   The donkey's dream.
Summary: A donkey has fantastic dreams while crossing the desert,
and at the end of the day the lady who has been riding on his back
gives birth in a cave to a very special baby, the baby Jesus.
1. Jesus Christ—Juvenile fiction. 2. Children's stories,
American. (1. Jesus Christ—Fiction.
2. Christmas—Fiction. 3. Donkeys—Fiction.
4. Dreams—Fiction) I. Title.
PZ7.B4513Do 1985   (Fic)   84-18905
ISBN 0-399-21233-7 (hardcover)
ISBN 0-399-22014-3 (Sandcastle paperback)
First Sandcastle Books impression

For my mother,
with love

Once there was a gray donkey. He was walking along as usual, with a load on his back. A man was leading him. And as they walked on and on through the starry night, the donkey began to dream.

He dreamed he was carrying a city,
with gates and towers and temple domes.

He dreamed a child cried in the city.
And doves flew all around.

He dreamed he was carrying a ship.

It rocked like a cradle. It shone like the moon.
And the sea danced all around.

He dreamed he was carrying a fountain.
Its waters splashed and sang like a child's laughter.

And a garden sprang from the desert sand all around.

He dreamed he was carrying a rose, soft as a
mother's touch and sweet as the sleep of a baby.

Angels stood all around.

Then he dreamed he was carrying a lady full of heaven.

They had come to a town. But only the village dogs
ran to greet them.

The man knocked on a door. It did not
open, so they had to go on. The donkey
followed him down narrow alleyways
paved with cobblestones.

They came to a place that smelled of hay,
with a watering trough and a cave for a stable.

The man helped the lady down from the donkey's back.
Then he took the donkey's saddle off and followed
the lady into the cave.

But the donkey was left alone outside.
He had walked so long, his back was
aching and his legs were sore. One star
high above him shone in the watering
trough below. The tired donkey drank.

Just then, a cry rang out in the cave.
And its echo rang like a bell,
over the hills, all around. The night
was so still, even the stars heard it.
The man came out of the cave.
He whispered to the donkey, "Come."

Together, they went inside the cave, where the lady lay
on a bed of hay. The donkey's saddle was her pillow.

She smiled. "Come," she said to the donkey.
"See what we have carried all this way, you and I."

It was only a tiny child. Yet, when the
baby opened his eyes, the cave was full
of light. The donkey blinked. But he
was not dreaming now. He was awake.

And suddenly, the donkey was not
tired anymore, though he had carried
a city, a ship, a fountain, a rose,
and all the heavens upon his back.

Author's Note

The Virgin Mary shares certain symbols with the universal "great mother." They have been given to her with special care, by tradition. In this book, the donkey dreams of some of them.

The city is a heavenly city, like the one in Revelation, full of promise and hope. On one of the Virgin's feast days, these words from a psalm are used: "Glorious things are said of you, O City of God."

From ancient times the ship has symbolized a womb and a cradle. This ship carries the Christ child to us across the sea. A medieval litany calls Mary "ark and ship and breeze and haven, moon and lamp and coming home."

Another litany calls her a "spiritual vessel." The fountain in the garden, an image that comes to Mary from the Song of Solomon, is such a vessel. This "well of living water" is also shaped like a chalice.

St. Bernard of Clairvaux called the Virgin Mary a flower. And the rose, queen of flowers, is her symbol. She is the rose of the world, the rose without thorns, and the "Rosa Mystica." In the heart of this mystic rose, the holy child is born.

Mary is also "Queen of Heaven." In paintings she is almost always robed in blue, the color of the heavens. The small blue flowers decorating the pages of this book are called forget-me-nots. When all the paintings were finished, I learned that a name for them in French is *les yeux de Marie*, Mary's eyes.

BHB